PUFFIN

SUPERPOWERS
THE HEADS OF HORROR

Books by Alex Cliff
SUPERPOWERS series

SUPER
THE HEADS OF HORROR
POWERS

ALEX CLIFF

ILLUSTRATED BY LEO HARTAS

PUFFIN

PUFFIN BOOKS

Published by the Penguin Group
Penguin Books Ltd, 80 Strand, London WC2R ORL, England
Penguin Group (USA) Inc., 375 Hudson Street, New York, New York 10014, USA
Penguin Group (Canada), 90 Eglinton Avenue East, Suite 700, Toronto, Ontario, Canada M4P 2Y3
(a division of Pearson Penguin Canada Inc.)
Penguin Ireland, 25 St Stephen's Green, Dublin 2, Ireland (a division of Penguin Books Ltd)
Penguin Group (Australia), 250 Camberwell Road, Camberwell, Victoria 3124, Australia
(a division of Pearson Australia Group Pty Ltd)
Penguin Books India Pvt Ltd, 11 Community Centre, Panchsheel Park,
New Delhi – 110 017, India
Penguin Group (NZ), 67 Apollo Drive, Rosedale, North Shore 0632, New Zealand
(a division of Pearson New Zealand Ltd)
Penguin Books (South Africa) (Pty) Ltd, 24 Sturdee Avenue, Rosebank,
Johannesburg 2196, South Africa

Penguin Books Ltd, Registered Offices: 80 Strand, London WC2R ORL, England

puffinbooks.com

Published 2007

3

Text copyright © Alex Cliff, 2007
Illustrations copyright © Leo Hartass, 2007
All rights reserved

The moral right of the author and illustrator has been asserted

Set in Bembo
Typeset by Palimpsest Book Production Limited, Grangemouth, Stirlingshire
Made and printed in England by Clays Ltd, St Ives plc

British Library Cataloguing in Publication Data
A CIP catalogue record for this book is available from the British Library

ISBN: 978-0-141-32134-9

www.greenpenguin.co.uk

To James, Edward and Nicholas Chapman

CONTENTS

JUST IMAGINE . . .

a ruined and crumbling castle on a grassy hillside surrounded by a deep dark moat.

As the sun's rays fall on the one remaining tower, a loud grinding noise shatters the silence and a section of the tower's thick inner wall begins to crumble. The noise fades and the dust clears, leaving a rectangular hole.

Two hands grip the edge of the hole and a man looks out of the wall. Deep wrinkles appear to be carved into his face and his hair is long and tangled. His heavy-lidded golden eyes look across the keep to the gatehouse opposite.

Six magical pictures glow in the stones around the arched castle gateway – a pair of wings, an arrow, a shield, a tree with an acorn, a leaping stag and a lion. They are traced in lines of burning white fire.

'My powers!' the man shouts despairingly to the sky.

As the words leave his mouth a jagged bolt of lightning rips down. The man instinctively shuts his eyes against the blinding light. When he opens them

again a woman is standing beside him.
But this is no ordinary woman. This is
the goddess Juno. As tall as two normal
people, her dark hair is piled up on her
head and a cloak of brown-grey feathers
swirls around her. She looks at the
trapped superhero.

'Yes, Hercules. Your lost superpowers.' Her black eyes flick to the gatehouse wall. 'Speed, accuracy, size-shifting, defence, agility and courage. Yesterday, your first superpower – strength – was

won back for you, but I still hold the other six powers and until you get them back you will remain my prisoner in this tower.' She looks at him mockingly. 'And your only hope is that two pathetic human boys can help you.'

Hercules thumps the walls of his prison. 'No! I will *not* have those two boys risk their lives for me again.'

Juno laughs. 'You have no choice. They made a deal with me. If they can complete the remaining six of the seven tasks I set them yesterday, all your powers will return.'

'And if they fail?' the superhero demands.

Juno's voice is as cold as the deepest sea. 'They die.'

'No!' Hercules exclaims.

The goddess leans closer to him. 'Accept it, Hercules. They agreed to the deal and now they must complete the tasks.'

Hercules glares at her. 'But they get

to choose one superpower each day to help them with each task.'

'They do.' An evil smile spreads across Juno's face. 'But you know as well as I that, even with a superpower, it is impossible that they will succeed. They are ordinary human boys. They won your strength back yesterday by mere luck.' The goddess twirls a lock of her dark hair gloatingly. 'Today they will fail.' Turning her head, she looks towards the path that leads to the castle. 'Listen. They are coming, Hercules. I can hear them.'

'No,' Hercules whispers.

'Oh yes!' Juno says. 'Now it is time for them to meet their fate.' She claps her hands together. 'The Nine-Headed River Monster awaits them!' A crash of thunder shakes the castle walls and the next instant she has gone.

High overhead a hawk cries out mockingly and a single brown-grey feather floats down through the sky.

CHAPTER ONE

THE CHOICE

Finlay charged down the stairs.
Reaching the third from the bottom
step at maximum speed, he leapt from
it, clearing his younger sister's Furby in
one easy bound. He skidded to a halt
on the wooden floor right next to
where his older sister, Jasmine, was
adjusting her hair in the hall mirror.

'Where are you off to, Fin?' she asked

as he grabbed his coat. 'Oh yeah. You've got that half-term football course on at school this morning, haven't you?'

'Later on,' Finlay replied, shoving his arms in the sleeves of his coat. 'Max and I have got stuff to do first.'

'What sort of stuff?' Jasmine asked curiously.

Finlay wondered what his older sister would say if he told her the truth. What would happen if he said: 'Well, actually, Jasmine, Max and I have got to go to the castle on the hill because the superhero Hercules has been magically imprisoned in the walls of the tower there by the evil goddess Juno. We're going to help him get his superpowers back. Yesterday we captured a sabre-toothed lion that Juno had set loose in the woods and got back his super-strength. Today we've got to get another superpower back for him by killing a nine-headed river monster.' What would Jasmine say to that?

'What sort of stuff?' Jasmine repeated curiously.

Finlay grinned. At the moment, this was his and Max's secret. 'Just stuff.' He turned the door handle. He'd overslept and was really late already. 'See ya!'

'Not so fast, Finlay.' Mrs Yates, their mum, appeared in the hall. 'I'd like you to explain this!' She held out a trainer. It had several long rips running from the top of it to the bottom and it was covered in puncture marks. 'I found it in your bedroom.'

Finlay's heart sank. 'I . . . um . . . I tore it a bit yesterday.'

'A bit!' Mrs Yates exclaimed. 'It looks like a dog's been savaging it!'

Finlay thought of the enormous sabre-toothed lion that had grabbed it and spat it out the day before. 'It wasn't a dog,' he said honestly.

His mum looked cross. 'You have to learn to be more careful. You're eight years old now, old enough to be responsible for your things . . .'

Finlay let his mum chunter on. His thoughts were far away from being careful. What was the river monster going to be like? How big was it going to be? What superpower would they choose to help them? Excitement swept through him. The day before, Max had got to be super-strong, which meant that today he definitely wanted to be the one who got the superpower. He'd stayed awake late into the night thinking about which power he'd choose, which was why he'd ended up oversleeping. He glanced at his watch. Oops, Max would have been waiting ages.

'Are you listening to me, Finlay?' his mum demanded suspiciously.

'Er . . . yeah,' Fin said quickly. 'I've

got to be more careful and do as I'm told,' he guessed, knowing that this was usually what his mum told him. 'Can I go to Max's now, Mum?'

His mum sighed. 'Oh, go on then, but remember that the football course starts at school at nine. Don't be late.'

Finlay nodded and, grabbing his kit bag, dashed thankfully out of the house. The church clock was striking half past eight now. That hardly left him and Max any time to get to the castle and speak to Hercules before getting to school for football.

I wish I could run faster, he thought as he dodged round an old lady walking at a snail's pace with a very old golden retriever dog. He took the short cut down the footpath that led behind the church. A cat leapt out of the way with a surprised miaow as he hurtled past.

Max was waiting for him by the gate to his house, kicking his football impatiently against the wall. 'What took you so long?' he exclaimed, picking up his ball and shoving it into his bag. 'We'd better move it. Remember, Hercules can only see out of the tower wall for twenty minutes each morning before the bricks come back over his face and he's gone for the day. If we don't get there in time we won't be able to pick up a superpower!'

'Sorry,' Finlay panted. 'I overslept, then Mum started telling me off. She found my trainer.'

Max pulled a face. 'Not good.'

'No,' Finlay agreed as they started to

run along the street together. 'She was really mad.'

'My mum kicked up a fuss about this.' Max showed Finlay his hand. On the back of it there was a deep cut, its edges still red with fresh blood, where one of the sabre-toothed lion's teeth had caught him. 'I had to say I did it while climbing a tree. Don't know what she'd have said if I'd told her it was a sabre-toothed lion!'

They stopped at the edge of the pavement. As a couple of cars went past, Finlay looked at Max's cut more closely. 'It's a strange shape — it looks like a hammer, doesn't it?'

'Yeah,' Max agreed. He looked quite pleased. 'Mum reckons it'll turn into a proper scar.'

'Cool,' said Finlay. The road was clear now. 'Come on! Let's move it!'

The dark waters of the moat glittered as Max and Finlay raced over the bridge to the castle. Usually there were

ducks paddling from one side to the other, but today the waters were deserted.

'I hope we're not too late,' Max panted as they scrambled through the gatehouse.

They ran into the castle's grassy inner keep. Relief flooded through Finlay as he looked at the tower and saw Hercules staring out desperately. 'It's OK. There's Hercules!' He swung round to look at the gatehouse entrance and saw six pictures burning in the stone. 'The symbols are there too.'

'Boys!' Hercules' voice rang across the keep. 'You have come.'

'Of course,' Max said, crossing the short grass. 'Did you think we wouldn't?'

'I was not sure. It is a very brave thing to do,' Hercules told them. 'You could still call the deal off. I can get Juno to come here and tell her that you have changed your minds. The Nine-Headed River Monster is deadly: it can strike from all directions. Even a practised swordsman would have little chance against it and you are just boys.'

Finlay felt a shiver of fear but he forced it away. 'We fought the Nemean Lion yesterday,' he pointed out bravely. 'We're going to fight this monster today and kill it and get you your powers back.'

'Yeah,' Max said stoutly.

'But this is madness!' Hercules protested.

'Well, we're doing it.' Finlay looked at

Max. 'Are we going to take it in turns
to have a superpower each day?'

Max nodded. 'OK.'

Finlay felt excitement beat through
him. 'Then it's my turn to get one
today!'

He began running towards the
gatehouse wall, his eyes fixed on the
symbols. Which one was he going to
choose? *Super-speed*, he decided,
thinking about how he'd felt when
running to meet Max. Being super–fast
would be brilliant!

'Wait!' Hercules called urgently.

Finlay stopped.

'If you must do this then it is
important that you choose correctly,'
Hercules said. 'To defeat the river
monster you must put your hand on

the arrow and choose accuracy. It is the
only power that I think will enable you
to defeat the monster.'

Finlay felt a stab of disappointment.
Accuracy didn't sound as much fun as

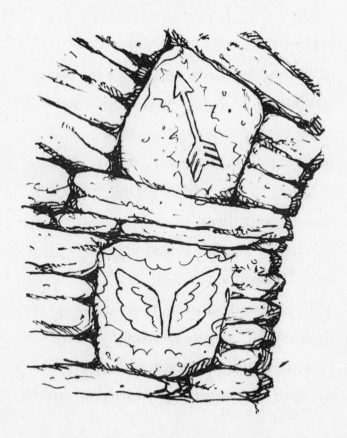

being super-fast. He looked at the arrow and then at the wings, which were the symbol for speed. *If I had super-speed I'd be able to run so fast it would be like flying*, he thought. *It would be like being Dash in* The Incredibles.

He hesitated. Hercules had told him to choose accuracy. But surely it would be good to be super-fast if he was facing a nine-headed monster? He'd be able to get out of the monster's way when it tried to attack him. He ran up to the gatehouse arch and looked from the wings to the arrow. Should he take Hercules' advice or follow his own feelings?

'Choose wisely, boy!' Hercules' voice echoed across the keep.

'I am doing,' Finlay whispered. And making his mind up he ran forward and banged his hand down on the burning white wings . . .

CHAPTER TWO

TOO LATE!

'No!' Finlay heard Hercules exclaim as the warmth flooded from the magic symbol into his hand. It tingled up his arm and spread through his whole body. After a few moments the stone under his fingers went cold. Finlay lifted his hand away. The symbol had gone.

'Hey!' he breathed as he turned slowly round. His body felt incredibly light, almost as if he might float away into the sky at any moment. A wave of giddiness hit him and he had to blink.

'Are you OK, Fin?' Max called.

'What have you done, boy?' Hercules' voice rang out in dismay as Finlay nodded and walked towards the tower. 'I told you to choose accuracy!'

Finlay looked at Hercules' shocked face. 'I know, but I just thought having speed might be useful,' he said. He looked down and kicked his foot against the grass. Now he had to explain himself to the superhero, suddenly choosing speed didn't seem such a great thing to have done. 'At least I'll be able to get away from the monster,' he said hopefully.

'But you're not supposed to get away

from it – you're supposed to kill it!'
Hercules stared at him despairingly.
'How can you hope to do that with
speed?'

'Um, I'll think of a way,' Finlay said.

'So are you super-fast now?' Max
demanded.

'Guess there's only one way to find
out,' replied Finlay. 'Got your watch?'

Max nodded; he had a stopwatch
function on his watch.

'Why don't you time how long it
takes me to run round the castle?'
Finlay said.

'Good idea.' Max punched the
buttons on his watch to set it up. His
fingers waited, poised over the start
button. 'OK.' The air shimmered for a
second where Finlay stood.

'Well?' demanded Finlay.

Max frowned. 'Well, what?'

'How fast was that?' Finlay said.

'How fast was what?' Max asked.

'That!'

Max looked at Finlay as if he'd gone
mental. 'What do you mean?'

'How long did it take me to run
round the castle?'

'You didn't . . .' Max started to say
but then his eyes widened. 'You ran
round the castle?'

Finlay nodded.

'But that was quicker than I could
even see,' Max told him. 'I didn't even
know you'd gone. You *really* ran all the
way round the castle?'

'Yeah,' Finlay replied. 'I'll do it again.
Watch.' He set off, racing round the
castle walls. The air blurred around him.
It was like going on a super-fast roller
coaster at the fair. The next second he
was back standing by Max. 'There!'

'That is *so* cool!' Max breathed. 'You

were back before I could even press the buttons! You really are super-fast!'

They exchanged high fives in delight.

A groan from Hercules made them swing round. He was holding his head in his hands. 'You will never defeat the river monster – never!' He sounded so full of despair that Finlay felt sorry for him.

'It'll be OK, Hercules,' he said bravely. 'I bet we can think of some way of using super-speed to help us.' A thought struck him. 'I can't wait to see what happens this morning; just think how fast I'll be when we're playing football!'

'You must keep the power secret,' Hercules said urgently. 'Or the deal will not stand. Remember what Juno said when she set the tasks yesterday?'

The boys looked blank.

'If you complete each task successfully *on your own*, then that power will return to me,' Hercules reminded them. 'You must not let anyone know of your power and you must not let anyone know about me in case they interfere. Now listen . . .' His tone became anxious as he looked at the sun. 'My time is running out today. You have acted foolishly in choosing the power of speed, but maybe all is not lost. Maybe I can come up with a plan.' His forehead furrowed as he thought hard. 'Yes, perhaps . . .'

'What we really need are some weapons,' Finlay interrupted him.

'Yeah,' Max agreed.

'A weapon is indeed important,'

Hercules said. 'And I can help. Listen carefully.' The boys stepped closer. 'When I was imprisoned, Juno placed my sword . . .'

There was a loud crunching noise. The stones started to close up in front of Hercules' face.

'Wait!' Finlay exclaimed.

'You will find it . . .' Hercules gasped, but before he could say any more the last stones re-formed in front of him, shutting him in.

Finlay couldn't believe it. 'He was about to say where his sword was! That's not fair! Hercules! Hercules!' he shouted, banging on the castle wall. But there was no answer. The wall was solid stone once more. The superhero had gone.

'What are we going to do now?' demanded Max.

'We'll just have to think of something else to use,' Finlay replied. He suddenly realized something. 'Hang on, no one's told us where to find this monster, Max.'

Max frowned. 'You're right. Where do you think it is?'

'Dunno,' Finlay replied. 'It could be in any bit of water that's big enough, I guess.'

'Oh, great,' Max groaned. 'So now we've got to fight a monster, with no weapon, and we don't even know where it is!'

Suddenly there was the sound of church bells ringing faintly in the village.

'Oh no!' Max said, looking at his watch. 'It's nine o'clock! We're going to be late for football!'

'But what about finding the monster?' exclaimed Finlay.

Max hesitated. 'If we don't go to football, Mr Roberts will tell our

mums and we'll get into loads of
trouble.'

Finlay felt torn. If his mum found out
he'd missed the football course she
probably wouldn't let him go out all
half-term and then there'd be no more
helping Hercules! But he so wanted to
find the monster . . .

'We have to go, Finlay!' Max said
urgently.

Finlay nodded. 'Yeah.' He broke into
a run. The world whizzed by. Castle
walls, the moat, trees and houses all
sped past . . .

Houses! Finlay stopped dead. He had
run so fast that he was now standing in
the middle of the village with the
school just in front of him. But where
was Max?

'Oh no,' he muttered as he suddenly realized that Max was probably still up by the castle.

He turned and ran back. It was a very strange feeling. His brain seemed to take over, telling his feet where to go without him having to think about it at all. The wind whistled in his ears. This was cool!

He reached the castle just in time to see Max running down the hill shouting, 'Fin! Wait!'

'I'm here.'

Max swung round and gaped. 'How did you get behind me?'

'I ran down to the village and back,' Finlay said. 'I got there in about three seconds!'

Max was very impressed. 'Wow!'

'We'd better go!' Finlay urged. 'Mr Roberts is going to go mad if we're late.'

Max looked worried. 'You go on ahead. It's stupid for us both to get into trouble.'

'No way! I can't leave you to get into trouble,' Finlay protested.

'You have to,' Max told him. 'Go on . . .'

But Finlay suddenly had an idea. 'No! I know what. I can give you a piggyback!' He appeared at Max's side almost before Max had blinked. 'Get on!'

Max hesitated. He was taller than Finlay. 'But . . .'

'Just get on!' Finlay told him, bending down. Max gave in. Grabbing Finlay round the neck, he scrambled on to his back. 'Oof!' Finlay exclaimed, his knees buckling.

'I'm too big. You can't do this,' Max said, beginning to loosen his grip.

'Oh yes I can!' Finlay said

determinedly. And not giving Max a
chance to get off, he began to run.
Within a few strides he had picked
up speed.

'Oh, wow!' Max gasped as the world
blurred around him. They hurtled into
the village and down the streets. Max
bumped around on Finlay's back,
clinging on to his neck as they charged
in through the school gates and into
the playground. The church bell gave a
last clang as Fin stopped. Losing his
balance, he half fell to his knees and
Max pitched off his back on to the
hard ground.

'Ooof!' he gasped.

'Sorry,' Fin panted.

'Finlay Yates!' A teacher's voice
snapped out. 'Max Hayward!'

Finlay and Max's heads shot up. Mr Roberts, their teacher, was standing in the school doorway, dressed in a black tracksuit and with a whistle around his neck. He stared at them sprawled on the ground in astonishment.

'Whatever do you two think you are doing?'

CHAPTER THREE

WHERE IS THE MONSTER?

Finlay and Max struggled to their feet. 'We're just practising our tackles,' Max said.

'Yes, rugby tackles,' added Finlay.

Mr Roberts frowned. 'Well, you're here to play football, not rugby, and you should be getting changed, not rolling around in the playground. Inside now, boys!'

Finlay and Max hurried into school. Their friends were all getting changed into their football gear.

'Thought you weren't coming,' George said as they began pulling off their coats.

'Oversleep, did you?' Matthew, George's twin brother, asked.

'Sort of,' muttered Max, swapping looks with Finlay.

Mr Roberts blew his whistle. 'OK, everyone! Outside and we'll start with two laps of the playground.' He fixed his gaze on Max and Finlay. 'One minute, then I want to see the pair of you outside too – or it'll be three laps.'

Max looked at Finlay. 'You could do three laps in three seconds!'

'But if Mr Roberts finds out I'm super-fast, it could ruin everything for Hercules,' Finlay realized. 'Maybe I shouldn't have chosen super-speed today after all.'

As everyone trooped outside Max

and Finlay quickly pulled on their shorts.

'What are we going to do?' Max said. 'We've got a monster to kill before sunset. We don't even know where it is at the moment and we've got to stay here for two hours!'

'Or maybe we don't,' Finlay said, thinking fast. 'I could use my super-speed to race off and see if I can find the monster. If I'm quick I bet Mr Roberts won't even notice I've gone!'

Max frowned. 'It's risky. I know you're fast, but you'll probably be gone for ages if you have to look for the monster.'

Fin squared his shoulders. 'I'll take the risk.'

★

It felt very strange going out to join their friends. George and Matthew were discussing the weekend's Chelsea versus Arsenal match. Amy and Anna were talking about a new pony at the riding stables they went to. It seemed impossible that everything was so normal. Finlay was filled with an incredible urge to shout at them all, 'I've got a superpower! I'm the fastest boy in the world!'

But actually he didn't need to shout it. He soon found out that it was very hard for him *not* to run super-fast. Even as he thought about how he would like to tell everyone about his super-speed, his legs speeded up and suddenly he was racing halfway round the playground and passing George and

Matthew. He hastily slowed down and looked around. To his relief, Mr Roberts was checking his watch and hadn't noticed that one of his pupils had achieved a new school record.

George and Matthew had though.

They ran up to him, open-mouthed.

'How did you do that?' George exclaimed.

Max ran past looking very worried.

Finlay thought fast. 'The, er, wind blew me along.'

'What wind?' George frowned.

'*This* wind!' Finlay made a rude noise. 'I had two tins of beans for breakfast!'

'Ugh, gross!' said Matthew.

'You should see how fast I go after three tins!' Finlay grinned. 'And how gross I smell!' He made another, even longer, rude noise and held his nose. Just as he'd hoped, George and Matthew burst out laughing, both forgetting about his burst of speed. They held their noses too.

Mr Roberts noticed them mucking

about. 'No stopping over there! On you go!'

Finlay thankfully carried on running. He found if he tried to keep his own feet in time with George and Matthew's he could just about manage to run at normal speed. 'Left, right, left, right, left, right,' he repeated under his breath.

But it was hard to concentrate all the time. His thoughts kept drifting to the monster. Where was it? There was a reservoir in the hills, maybe it was there? Or in the river in the woods? Or in the lake by the caravan site . . .

The next instant he found himself shooting on ahead. He had to race all the way round the playground, coming back to rejoin George and Matthew.

Luckily he was so fast this time they didn't even realize he'd gone.

By the time he had done this five times, he was very glad when they finished their supposed two laps and Mr Roberts called them into the middle.

'Line up in two teams!' the teacher called, placing two rows of cones up the playground. 'First person in each team has to dribble a ball round these cones and back to their team, then the next person can go and the next. The first team with everyone back is the winner.'

There were exactly eleven of them in each team. 'I reckon the monster could be in the reservoir,' Finlay whispered to Max as they joined the end of their team's line.

'This could be your chance, Fin,'

Max said under his breath. 'You could go and check it before your turn in the game. Mr Roberts will be too busy to notice.'

Finlay checked round. Everyone was looking at Mr Roberts, waiting for him to blow the whistle. 'Here goes!' he said and he set off.

The village whistled by – houses, gateways, the village shop, the church. Almost before he knew it, he was out on the roads, whizzing up into the hills where the reservoir was. This was brilliant! He was like a human rocket! A real life super-boy!

Suddenly he realized that the track around the reservoir was just ahead of him. He skidded to a stop and looked about.

The reservoir spread out in front of
him – an enormous expanse of still
water. To Finlay's relief there was no
one there. He stared down at the water.
It looked perfect for a river monster to
hide in. Picking up a large stone he ran
to the water's edge and chucked it as

far as he could. It fell with a splash, ripples spreading out away from where it had sunk. Finlay held his breath. What was he going to do if a monster erupted from the water?

Run, he told himself.

He waited.

Nothing.

Finlay waited for a few more moments and then tried chucking another stone. Still nothing. But how could he be sure? The reservoir was very large. The monster might be hiding under the water over on the other side.

As he stared at the flat surface of the water he remembered a scene from *The Incredibles* when Dash had run across the water.

I could run across the reservoir, Finlay thought. *If the monster's hiding underneath I bet it'll come out to see what's happening if it sees my feet!*

It might also bite my feet . . .

He pushed away the horrible thought and ran straight towards the reservoir. In a second he was on the water. It felt like running on wobbly jelly. It was weird but fun. He charged back and forward from one side of the reservoir to the other.

'Hey, monster!' he called.

Nothing happened.

Feeling a mixture of disappointment and relief Finlay ran off the water and on to the far bank. The monster couldn't be in the reservoir. He was sure it would have appeared if it was hiding there. And he knew he couldn't afford to hang around any longer or he'd be missed at school. Turning round he ran back as fast as he could.

He arrived in the playground just as Max reached the front of the queue.

Everyone was yelling out names and clapping their hands, as they encouraged their teams on. Luckily no one apart from Max seemed to notice Finlay reappear.

'Did you find the monster?' Max hissed as Finlay arrived beside him.

Finlay shook his head. 'It must be somewhere else!' he gasped as George returned and Max took his turn with the ball.

The next exercise involved them working in pairs and taking it in turns to tackle each other. Max and Finlay retreated to the quietest corner of the playground.

'Shall I go and look for the monster again?' Finlay said. 'I could try the lake by the campsite!'

Max nodded. 'If Mr Roberts asks where you are I'll say you've gone to the toilet.'

Finlay set off. He tried the lake and then the river in the woods, but there was no sign of the monster at either place.

He got back, puffing and panting, his hair sticking up, just as Mr Roberts came over. 'You two look like you've been working hard,' he said, looking at Finlay's red face. 'Good lads! We'll have a match now. Hope your shooting's up to its usual form, Max.'

Blowing on his whistle, he called everyone into the middle. They split into their teams. 'We'd better stop looking for the monster now,' Max whispered as everyone got into position.

'Mr Roberts is bound to notice if you disappear in the middle of a game.'

'But we've got to find it!' Finlay said urgently. 'We don't want to be wasting time this afternoon when we should be trying to kill it. I'll go and try the river up by Symthes's farm.'

'Don't,' Max hissed. 'The game's about to start . . .' But he was too late. Finlay had already gone!

CHAPTER FOUR

GOAL!

The whistle went. Max looked round in alarm. The game had started! He felt his heart beating fast. What if Mr Roberts noticed Finlay was missing?

Luckily it was a quick game and Max was soon caught up in the action. After a few minutes George got the ball and raced towards the goal, but finding his way blocked by defenders, George turned and passed back to Max. Anna and Amy closed Max down, forcing him to cross it to Matthew. Harvey raced in to tackle Matthew. Matthew looked to pass the ball back to an unmarked player.

'Where's Fin?' he shouted.

Mr Roberts glanced round.

Max's stomach tightened with fear. No! Mr Roberts mustn't realize Fin wasn't there. 'To me, Matthew!' he yelled, pelting towards the right wing and leaving Fraser, who was marking him, way behind.

Matthew fired the ball in his direction.

Max whisked round with it and set off towards the goal. He was clear, just the goalie to beat.

'Shoot!' yelled everyone in his team.
From the corner of his eye Max
could see Mr Roberts looking on in
confusion. He was sure the teacher
had realized Finlay was missing. He

had to do something to cause a distraction.

He hesitated for a second and then, swinging his leg back, he booted the ball high and wide into the bushes.

Max's team all groaned.

'Oh, Max!' George exclaimed.

'How *could* you miss!' cried Edward.

'That was the easiest goal in the world!' Matthew said.

Max looked at them apologetically but his tactic had worked. Mr Roberts was distracted. He blew his whistle. 'Can you go and find the ball, please, Anna?' He came over to Max, looking at him in surprise. 'Not on form today, Max? It's not like you to miss the target.'

Max felt awful. He'd let his whole

team down and he hated Mr Roberts
looking at him like that. He was usually
the team's star striker. He wandered
down the pitch, looking around. Where
was Finlay? Any minute now Mr
Roberts was going to realize that he
wasn't here.

He felt a movement in the air and
Finlay appeared at his side, gasping for
breath.

'Fin!' Max exclaimed. 'You were ages!
Did you find the monster?'

Finlay shook his head. 'Did Mr
Roberts notice I wasn't here?'

'Almost.' Max quickly filled him in
on what had been happening as Anna
came back with the ball and everyone
got ready for the goal kick. 'We can't
risk it again.'

Finlay nodded. 'Sorry about you having to muck up the shot.'

'It's OK.' Max tried to look like he didn't care.

Finlay wasn't fooled. 'I'll make it up to you,' he promised. 'You'll see.'

Finlay soon found that while he couldn't safely use his super-speed while others were watching him dribbling the ball, it did mean that he had no problem at all in losing Emily, his marker. All he had to do was drift behind her and put on a super-quick burst of speed while she wasn't watching. Max finally realized what he was doing and the next time he saw Finlay clear on the wing he decided to take a chance. As soon as he had passed the ball to the right, Max sprinted straight at the goal. By the time he got there Fin had kicked the ball across. It was high, but Max was ready.

'Gotcha!' he said, chesting the ball down, and shooting it cleanly into the net.

His team all cheered.

'Great goal!' Mr Roberts shouted approvingly.

Max glowed with pride.

Finlay ran over and they exchanged high fives. 'Told you I'd make it up to you!' he hissed.

'Thanks!' Max grinned.

The final whistle went.

'We've won!' George yelled, coming up and punching Max on the arm.

'That was a wicked goal!' Matthew said.

'Hope you play like that when we take on Burton school next week,' Amy said.

'Yeah, we'll slaughter them if you do!' Harvey said.

'Hope there is a next week,' Finlay muttered to Max as they hurried in to change.

'Me too,' said Max, thinking about the monster. He shivered. 'How are we going to find this thing, Fin?'

'Maybe we should go to the castle,' replied Finlay. 'There might be some clues – perhaps Juno left us a note or something.'

Max looked doubtful. 'She doesn't seem the sort to leave a note. Metre-high letters burnt in stone with lightning bolts maybe, but not a note!'

'Anything would do,' Fin sighed.

As soon as they had got changed they

picked up their kit bags and headed towards the door.

'Nice work today, boys,' Mr Roberts said. 'That was a great goal, Max. Finlay, you did very well too.' He nodded approvingly. 'You've got a nice turn of speed when you use it!'

Finlay wondered what would happen next time he and Max played football. He had a feeling Mr Roberts was going to be disappointed. Oh well. He pictured Max's killer goal flying into the back of the net. It had been worth it just to see that!

Calling goodbye to their friends, he and Max left school behind and hurried towards the castle.

'You go on ahead,' Max panted. 'See

if you can find any clues about where the monster is.'

Fin raced off up the track in a blur of light. Within seconds he was running across the dark moat. He ran to the tower. His eyes searched over the bricks. No note. No clue. Nothing. He began to search around the castle, but there was no sign of any message.

'Have you found anything?' Max called when he eventually appeared, huffing and puffing, in the castle entrance.

'No,' Finlay replied, frustrated. He climbed over the wall of the gatehouse towards the moat. 'I bet Juno wants us to fail and that's why she hasn't told us where the monster is.'

'I guess,' Max said, following him. The

grassy banks led down to the water. There were piles of duck poo but no ducks, Max noticed. *Weird*, he thought. *There were always ducks on the banks*. 'Where are the ducks, Fin?' he said.

But Finlay was too busy thinking about Juno to answer. 'It doesn't make sense,' he said slowly. 'We know Juno wants to see us get killed. So in that case she must want us to find the monster. So why hasn't she told us where it is? Unless . . .' He broke off as an idea popped into his head.

Max looked at the still waters of the moat. A large, circular ripple spread out across the water as if something had just moved beneath the surface. Further along the moat there was another ripple, and another . . .

Icy fingers ran down Max's spine. 'Finlay!' he said in a shaky voice. He began to back away up the bank.

'Unless the monster was somewhere she would expect us to find it easily.' Finlay turned to Max with mounting alarm. 'That's it! I bet the monster must be somewhere nearby like . . .'

'Behind you, Fin!' Max yelled.

Finlay whirled round as a tangle of green flesh exploded upwards out of the moat with an ear-splitting shriek.

'I think the monster got fed up waiting!' gasped Max. '*It's* found *us*!'

CHAPTER FIVE

THE RIVER MONSTER

The monster reared into the sky. Each
of its slimy round heads bobbed about
on the end of a fat scaly neck. A single
bloodshot eye the size of a dinner plate
sat in the centre of each horrible face.
As if acting under a single command,
the creature's many mouths snapped
open, revealing rows of jagged yellow
fangs.

The heads swayed in the air, their
terrible eyes fixing on the boys. The
monster let out a bloodcurdling shriek
of fury.

'Quick, Max!' Finlay yelled. 'Take
cover in the tower!'

He turned and a second later
reached the tower. As he stopped he
realized that Max was still down by the
water.

'No!' he gasped. He raced back just
in time to see a head swooping down
at Max like a snake striking at a
mouse.

'Watch out!' Finlay shouted. Grabbing
Max by the arm he yanked him out of
the way just in time. The monster's
fangs struck the ground just where Max
had been standing. And already another

three heads were shooting towards
them.

'Piggyback!' Finlay yelled.

Max didn't need telling twice. He
threw himself on to Finlay's back. Finlay
leapt forward and raced out of range.

'You OK?' Finlay panted as he and Max collapsed on the floor of the tower.

'Yeah,' Max gasped.

Finlay's heart was pounding so quickly he thought it was going to burst out of his chest. He peered shakily out of the tower doorway. The monster's heads were weaving above the castle walls, the horrible eyes raking across the castle grounds, searching for the boys.

'What are we going to do?' Max asked Finlay.

For once Finlay was out of ideas. 'I don't know.' He felt a wave of fear. Suddenly, thinking that they could kill the monster just like that seemed as dumb as imagining he could play football as well as he had today without his superpower. Maybe if they had a fighter jet or if they could blast it with mega machine guns they'd stand a chance but they had nothing. It was just them and it. And it had *nine* heads!

Behind them the monster screamed furiously.

'We're going to get ourselves killed if we go out there,' Max said shakily.

Fin nodded. 'But if we don't . . .'

They looked at each other, knowing what the other one was thinking. If they didn't kill the monster, Hercules wouldn't get his super-speed back and without it he'd never be able to break free from the tower. Juno would have won.

Max took a deep breath. 'We have
to try.'

Three of the monster's heads lashed
down towards the tower entrance.

Finlay leapt backwards from the
doorway. 'We have to find some

weapons!' he exclaimed. 'If only we knew where Hercules' sword was!'

Max looked round desperately. 'When he was talking about it he made it sound as if we could find it.'

Finlay looked at the wall where Hercules was imprisoned. If only they could talk to him, but the wall was just grey stone again, with a few holes where some stones had fallen out. 'Do you think it's in there with him?'

'Knowing Juno I bet she'll have put it somewhere just out of his reach,' Max replied.

'So, sort of, just about here maybe,' Finlay said, touching the wall a little way from where he judged Hercules' right hand might be.

The wall crumbled slightly and suddenly Finlay could feel a proper hole. The two boys looked at each other.

'You don't think . . .' Finlay caught his breath.

Just then, a head came swinging at the tower like a cannonball. It couldn't quite reach and pulled up sharp with a frustrated, ear-piercing shriek.

'Quick!' Max yelled to Finlay. 'Try!'

Finlay thrust his hand in the hole. The surrounding stone scraped at his skin but as he frantically wriggled his fingers he felt the stone start to break up even more and the hole got bigger. He reached in further. His hand touched something cold and hard.

'There's something in here!' he

gasped. 'Quick, let's see if we can get it out! Help me, Max!'

With the monster's screams echoing in their ears the two of them began to bang and push at the bricks around the hole. The stone magically crumbled to

dust under their fingers, leaving a long
rectangular hole running down the wall.
Peering into it, the boys saw a glint of
silver metal.

'Look!' Finlay breathed. Reaching in
with both hands he heaved out a heavy
broadsword. Its silver blade was
engraved with carvings of strange beasts
and monsters. Its hilt was made of gold
and encrusted with rubies.

'It weighs a ton,' he said. Bracing his
legs, he wrapped both of his hands
round the hilt. Suddenly the red rubies
began to glow. Warmth flooded into
Finlay's hands and he felt the sword's
weight magically seem to shift in
balance with his own. Leaning back on
his heels, he found he could lift it. He
raised it high into the air and then

swung it from left to right. His arms and the blade seemed to move as one as the sword cleaved through the air.

'Oh, wow!' he breathed.

'It doesn't look heavy to me,' Max yelped, dodging out of the way in alarm.

'It is. It just doesn't feel heavy when you lift it. It must be magic,' Finlay replied. 'I wonder how sharp it is.' He swung the sword towards a boulder lying on the floor. The blade sliced through the stone as cleanly as if it had been a light sabre.

'Wow!' Max exclaimed as the boulder fell into two halves. 'That's sharp!'

Outside three more heads swung at the tower doorway, fangs snapping hungrily.

'Sharp enough to cut off nine heads?' Finlay said.

'Guess there's only one way to find out!' Max exclaimed.

A grin spread across Finlay's face. He shifted the sword into one hand and pointed it at the door. 'Let's go kill a monster!'

CHAPTER SIX

THUNK!

Finlay strode out of the tower. Max ran after him, asking, 'So what's the plan?'

'I'm going to use my super-speed to run so fast the monster won't be able to see me and then I'll cut off all its heads,' Finlay declared.

Max was impressed. 'Cool!'

The monster's heads swung round the

castle keep on their scaly green necks. There were so many of them! Finlay's heart skipped a beat and for a moment his footsteps slowed. *I can do this*, he told himself, tightening his grip on the sword. *I have to!*

The monster's dreadful eyes swivelled towards him. A head whipped downwards.

'Fin!' Max gasped, darting back into the tower.

'Here goes!' Finlay yelled. He charged forward to meet it. Jaws open, fangs gleaming, it swung at him. He could see the green scales on the neck, the red thread-like veins that streaked across the yellow eyeball. The monster's shriek filled his ears, drowning out the pounding of his heart.

Finlay swung the sword back as if it were a rounders bat and slashed straight at the monster's neck.

Thunk!

The blade bit into bright-green scales. The force of the swing took it straight through the monster's neck and out the

other side. Green goo burst into the sky as the chopped-off head catapulted upwards.

'I did it!' Finlay yelled.

'Way to go!' Max shouted, from the shelter of the gatehouse.

The head thudded to the grass, the mouth open, the eye shut. Fin's breath was coming fast in his throat, his mind was buzzing. He'd cut off one of the monster's heads. Just eight more to go . . .

The air was filled with the sounds of furious screaming. Finlay saw that all the monster's other heads were snaking towards him.

With a burst of super-speed he charged forward, sword at the ready. He could do this!

Thunk! Another head catapulted into
the air. Courage raced through Fin as
he turned to face the next and the
next. *Thunk! Thunk! Thunk!* Heads
somersaulted upwards. Hot, sticky goo
spattered everywhere, covering Finlay's
face and arms, but he ignored it. *Thunk!
Thunk!*

The final head bore down on him
like a speeding train. Finlay's sword
whistled through the air. *Thunk!*

'Yay!' Finlay shouted in triumph as
the head thumped into the grass. All
the necks were waving above him,
headless now. 'I've done it . . .'

But then he paused, confused. If the
beast was beaten, why wasn't it dead
and still?

'Look at that neck!' Max's yell jerked

him out of his thoughts. He swung
round on the balls of his feet and
looked upwards. The neck of the first
head he had cut off was coiling above
him but something strange and horrible

was happening to it. Finlay stared. The scales around the cut seemed to be bubbling. They were moving and pulsing. Something football-shaped seemed to be pushing its way out through the skin.

With a loud shriek two new heads burst out of the neck, their mouths open, their eyes wide and glistening.

'Argh!' Finlay and Max both yelled.

All around them, each of the other necks sprouted two new heads too! They swooped at Finlay. Running forward in a blur of speed, he began cutting them off as fast as he could.

But it didn't matter how many he cut off, more always appeared.

'We need a new plan!' Max yelled.

Looking at the heads bursting out of

the necks in all directions, Finlay
agreed. He raced to the gatehouse.

Four heads struck at the gatehouse
roof. As their fangs crashed into it the
roof began to crumble.

'What are we going to do?' Max
exclaimed.

Finlay looked at the sword. 'We can't kill it by chopping off its heads. This sword is useless!'

'So why did Hercules try to tell us where to find it?' Max felt desperate. 'We must be able to use it in some way.'

'But how?' Finlay said. 'The more heads we chop off the more there are!'

He looked out of the gatehouse. The heads were swooping around the keep. Several times the long necks almost got tangled. Watching them gave him an idea. 'OK, how about this for a new plan?' he said quickly. I go out there and run round. I'll try and get the necks to tangle up and tie themselves in knots. Maybe it'll strangle itself.'

It didn't seem a great plan, but just

Thunk!

then another four heads crashed into the gatehouse roof. Stones crashed down around them.

'OK!' Max gasped, ducking to avoid the falling rubble. 'Anything's worth a try!'

CHAPTER SEVEN

THE MISSING HEAD

Finlay raced out of the gatehouse. The monster's eyes fixed on him and the heads moved as one. They reared upwards, poising themselves, ready to strike.

Max felt a wave of fear sweep over him. Feeling small and powerless, he found himself counting the monster's many heads. There were thirty-two in

total, bouncing about on eight thick
necks. How could Finlay possibly hope
to tangle them all up? Max frowned.
Eight necks? It was supposed to be a
nine-headed monster, at least at the
start! There should be *nine* necks.

Maybe I can't see one, he thought.

He edged out into the keep,
wondering if one of the necks would
come swooping towards him, but the
monster was too busy watching Finlay.
Max counted the necks. Definitely
eight. So where was the ninth?

He crept round the gatehouse wall. It
had to be here somewhere. He crept on
towards the moat. His hands felt sweaty.
At any moment he expected a hideous
head to rear up out of the water and
strike at him.

He stopped with a gasp. There, under the stone bridge, he could see the monster's bulky body almost completely submerged by water from which the eight necks were waving. There was the missing head and neck! The head on

this neck was enormous, much bigger than any of the other heads. It had a huge eye, black as a starless sky, and the skin all over it was pulsing in and out. Drool trickled out of the corner of its wide mouth.

Suddenly the monster's ninth head swivelled towards Max. Fear exploded through his brain as its terrible black eye seemed to stare straight at him. He froze, expecting it to rear up on a long neck and strike him down; but then to his surprise the eye swivelled onwards as if it hadn't seen him at all. And yet from the way it flickered around from side to side it seemed to be seeing *something* . . .

Max stared at it for a moment. It was almost as if the monster were watching something not right there in front of him; as if it were seeing through other eyes . . .

He had to tell Fin!

He edged as quietly as he could back up the bank to the gatehouse. Scrambling over the stones he burst out into the keep.

Five of the necks were tangled up and the other three were striking at Finlay. Two of them tied themselves in a knot as they chased Finlay around the grass.

'Gotcha!' Finlay shouted triumphantly. 'He saw Max. 'Just one more to go!'

'No, there isn't, Fin!' Max yelled. 'There's another head! It's under the drawbridge. It's enormous!'

Fin stared at him. 'What?'

The four heads on the remaining neck behind him swung down.

'Watch out!' Max yelled.

Finlay glanced round. Seeing the danger he turned to run, but even with his super-speed he wasn't quite fast enough. A fang caught his shoulder.

He yelled and stumbled in pain. As he fell to the ground he only just managed to avoid falling on to Hercules' sword. The heads whipped towards him. He rolled over and swung his sword at them. The neck swerved backwards before moving in to strike again.

Lying on his back Finlay slashed the sword upwards.

Max watched in horror as the four heads swept down, their eyes fixed on Fin. It was as if a single brain were controlling them . . .

That's it! The enormous head under the drawbridge flashed into Max's mind. *There* is *just one brain*, he realized. *And I bet it's in that huge head.*

He raced back through the gatehouse. If he could distract that big master-head then maybe Finlay would have a chance to get up and escape. But what could he use to distract the monster?

Suddenly he saw his kit bag on the bank. He'd abandoned it there when the monster had first appeared. There were just his clothes and a football in it though. How could they help him?

In his mind he saw the horrible head with its one huge eye. *A football* . . .

Maybe, just maybe . . .

Max snatched the football out of the bag. The enormous head was still under the bridge, its slimy green skin pulsing, its black eye swivelling excitedly. Max was now sure it was watching what was going on in the courtyard through the eyes on its other heads. So what would happen if this eye in front was forced shut?

He took his football out of the bag and for a moment he relived the goal from the match. Now the stakes were a million times higher – could he pull off another great shot like that, or would he bottle it?

There was no time to hesitate, no time even to think. He placed the ball at his feet.

'Take this!' he yelled.

He swung his leg back and took his shot. The ball torpedoed straight into the monster's big black eye. The head jerked as if it had been shot and thick yellow slime erupted from the eyeball. The massive mouth jerked open with a tree-shaking shriek.

From the other side of the wall Max could hear the sound of the other heads shrieking too. He scrambled up the bank and looked through the gatehouse window. His guess had been right. The heads that were knotted together were now thrashing wildly from side to side and the four heads that had been threatening Finlay were swinging through the sky. Their eyes were winking frantically as if they couldn't see. With the master-head blinded by pain, all the other heads were blind too.

Finlay scrambled to his feet, but the heads didn't notice.

Max raced to the wall.

'Finlay! There's another head here! Quick!'

Finlay began to run. In the blink of

an eye he appeared at Max's side, sword in his hand.

He gasped when he saw the head. It was thrashing about wildly on its short, stumpy neck.

'I bet that's where the brain is!' Max gasped.

'Not for much longer!' Finlay exclaimed.

Racing forward, he ran on to the water, heading straight at the monster. Lifting the sword, he swung it at the monster's neck. It sliced through in one clean motion. The enormous head flew upwards as Fin reached the far bank of the moat.

'You did it, Fin!' Max yelled as the other eight necks waving over the keep finally collapsed.

There was a blinding flash and then there was silence. Max and Fin looked at the drawbridge.

The monster had disappeared!

CHAPTER EIGHT

JUNO RETURNS

Finlay and Max stared at the moat, the
dreadful echo of the monster's screams
ringing in their ears.

'What – what happened?' stammered
Finlay.

'I think you killed it!' Max said. 'It's
gone!'

'The sword's vanished too!' Finlay
said, looking down at his empty hands.

'Ow!' he winced. 'My shoulder's hurting.'

Max looked at Finlay's shoulder. There was a tear in Fin's coat and jumper where the monster's fang had caught him.

Finlay shrugged off his coat and craned his neck but he couldn't see the wound. 'Does it look bad?' he asked.

'It's bleeding quite a lot,' Max said, inspecting the wound. 'But I think your coat must have protected you a bit. I bet it's going to turn into a scar though.' He frowned. 'It's a weird shape. There's a bit to the left and a bit to the right.'

'So we'll both have scars,' Finlay said. 'I hope it's not poisoned.' Suddenly he felt a strange swirling sensation in his chest. 'Something weird's happening to me, Max,' he said in alarm. The swirling got faster and faster. 'My heart feels like it's about to burst out of my chest.'

'It's not your heart,' Max told him, remembering the same sensation from the day before. 'It's the superpower!'

A golden light seemed to flood out of Finlay's chest. It streamed through the gatehouse and across the castle keep. Max and Finlay raced after it. Now the superpower had left Finlay, he struggled to keep up with Max. They reached the gatehouse entrance just in time to see the golden light hit the inner wall of the tower opposite.

There was a loud grinding noise and the stones hiding Hercules' face vanished.

'Boys! You have killed the Nine-Headed River Monster!' Hercules exclaimed. 'My power has come back!' His golden eyes glowed. He seemed to stand straighter and his hair looked thicker and less grey. 'How did you do it?'

'Finlay cut off the master-head with your sword. He was brilliant!' Max said.

'You were the one who found the master-head and blinded it with a football!' Finlay pointed out.

'But only after you'd distracted the other heads by tying them in knots,' Max added.

Hercules looked very confused. 'Knots? Footballs? What are you talking about, boys?'

'Well,' Max said. 'It happened like this . . .'

By the time he and Finlay had finished the story of how they had come to kill the monster, Hercules was shaking his head.

'I have never heard of anyone using a ball to defeat a river monster before. Your ways of defeating the creature were most unusual.' He looked at them with new respect in his eyes. 'Rather like you two boys, I'm beginning to think.'

Finlay and Max grinned at each other.

Crash!

A flash of lightning shot down from the sky. Finlay and Max jumped as Juno suddenly appeared in the centre of the tower.

'So,' she said, glaring at them down her long nose. 'You two worms have succeeded in completing the second task.'

'These boys have much to be proud of,' Hercules put in. 'They completed the task you set, and in doing so showed great resourcefulness, skill and courage.'

'Pah!' Juno exclaimed. 'They were lucky once again!' Her burning gaze raked across the boys. 'There are still five more tasks to go. Let us wait until tomorrow to see if there exists a crumb of skill in either of them.'

Finlay remembered what the next task
was. 'We've got to clean some really
dirty stables tomorrow, haven't we?'

'*Impossibly* dirty stables,' Juno
replied.

'At least there's no monster to fight,'
Max said.

The goddess's black eyes glinted. 'Nothing is ever as simple as it seems.'

Hercules looked at her in alarm. 'Juno, what have you got planned?'

'Patience, Hercules.' Juno looked at the boys. 'They will find out soon enough!' She laughed delightedly and clapped her hands. There was a crash of thunder and she vanished. In the same instant the stones in the wall closed up and Hercules disappeared.

Max and Finlay looked at each other.

'We'll be all right,' Max said. 'We killed a nine-headed monster today. I mean it's not like horse poo can be more scary than that!'

'Whatever Juno has waiting, we'll deal with it,' Finlay agreed. He lifted his hand in a high five. 'We'll get the better of her!'

'Yeah,' Max grinned, slapping his palm against Fin's. 'We will!'

High overhead, a hawk screamed as if it were laughing.

ABOUT THE AUTHOR

ALEX CLIFF LIVES IN A VILLAGE IN LEICESTERSHIRE, NEXT DOOR TO FIN AND JUST DOWN THE ROAD FROM MAX, BUT UNFORTUNATELY THERE IS NO CASTLE ON THE OUTSKIRTS OF THE VILLAGE. ALEX'S HOME IS FILLED WITH TWO CHILDREN AND TWO LARGE AND VERY SLOBBERY PET MONSTERS.

WILL MAX AND FIN SAVE HERCULES IN TIME?

HOW WILL THEY BEAT THE SCARIEST SMELL IN THE WORLD?

FIND OUT IN . . .

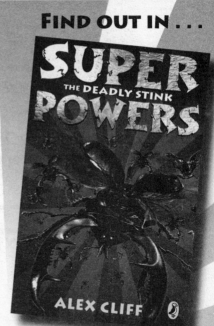

SUPER
THE DEADLY STINK
POWERS

ALEX CLIFF

DID YOU KNOW?

Hercules lived in Ancient Greece. He was the son of a woman named Alcmene and the god Zeus. When Hercules was a baby he could fight snakes with his bare hands! The labours he had to complete were originally set for him by his cousin Eurystheus, King of Mycenae.

THE HYDRA

The Hydra was a swamp-dwelling creature. It was a gigantic water snake with nine heads. These heads were indestructible – no matter how many times they were chopped off they grew back! Legend has it that even its breath could kill. It was said that Juno raised the Hydra so that it would one day attack Hercules. When Hercules went on this quest, he was aided by his trusty nephew Iolaus. It was only through teamwork that they defeated the monster.

YOUR
SUPER POWERS
QUEST

YOU NEED:

2 players
2 counters
1 dice
and nerves of steel!

YOU MUST:

Collect all **seven** superpowers
and save Hercules, who has
been trapped in the castle by
the evil goddess, Juno. All you
have to do is roll the dice and
follow the steps on the books
– try not to land on Juno's rock
or one of the monsters!

JOIN THE QUEST!
COLLECT ALL 7 BOOKS AND PLAY THE SUPERPOWERS GAME

❶ You need a **SUPERPOWER** to save Hercules, off you go!

❸ You've got today's power – strength! MOVE FORWARD THREE ROCKS

❼ YOWSERS! You've left the hammer behind. MISS A GO

START

❷ OH NO! You've landed on Juno's rock. Back to the start!

❻ RUN FASTER! It's getting closer. ROLL AGAIN

❽ GO! You're only six powers from saving Hercules, GO TO THE NEXT QUEST!

❹ EEK! Time is running out, but you can't move until you roll a three.

❺ YIKES! You must brave the Jaws of Doom. RUN ACROSS TWO ROCKS

PUFFIN
puffinbooks.com

U.K. £3.99
CAN. $0.00

ISBN 978-0-141-32133-9

YOU CAN:

PLAY BOOK BY BOOK

The game is only complete when all seven books in the series are lined
up. But if you don't have them all yet, you can still complete the quests!
Whoever lands on the 'GO' rock first is the winner of that particular quest.

PLAY THE WHOLE GAME

Whoever collects all seven superpowers and is first to land on the final
rock has completed the entire quest and saved Hercules!

REMEMBER:

If you land on a 'Back to the Start' symbol, don't worry – you don't have
to go all the way back to book one – just back to the start of the game
on the book you are playing.

GOOD LUCK, SUPERHEROES!

puffin.co.uk